W0396674

Broken Hearts Only

poetry by
Brandon Helms

Dedicated to the memory of my father. You were the reason I had the courage to pursue my dreams. I will never forget you or your love for me.

chapter one

heartbreak

if only we could listen
to each other
perhaps then humanity
would not be so messed up

-humanity

there is nothing
so tragic
as thinking
someone
was so perfect for you

and yet
they won't
love you back

-unrequited love

no one is perfect

we just have to find someone
whose flaws
are worth loving

-worth loving

we spend so much time
chasing after glitter
that we neglect the gold
beneath our own feet

-tunnel vision

if you have to convince someone
to spend time with you
or love you

they aren't worth your time.

-and they never will be

sometimes it's just easier
to curl up in a ball
and cry

-waterfalls

i am tired of giving my everything
to someone who doesn't notice
my efforts

-time for change

it's hard realizing
that someone you cared about
only came into your life
to use you

-being used is never a good feeling

just because
someone
once hurt you

doesn't mean
that everyone
who comes
after them

also will.

-some things change

don’t waste your time
on inconsistent people

consistency
is so hard to find
these days

everyone
treats you one way
one day
and the next day
another way

-consistent

to everyone
who has survived
dark situations
and low points
in life:

take a moment
to breathe
and congratulate yourself

for you have proved your strength
you have made it through
and you
can handle
anything
life
throws
at you.

-survivors

there will
always be
those
certain people
who feel
like home

-you feel like home to me

don’t believe the lies
people tell
just to keep you around

-you are more valuable than that

it is all too easy
to hate yourself
for falling short

but never forget
that everyone
has fallen short;
even your heroes

so don't be
so hard on yourself

-let yourself make mistakes

there is nothing
quite as difficult
as having
to start
all over
again

-square one

never give up
you have come too far
and fought too hard
to give up now

-hold on

i have wasted
too many tears
on people
who don't care
as much as i do

-*wasted tears*

every ‘i love you’
was a lie

i wish i could have seen that
before it was too late

-lies

he may have broken you
but your love
for yourself
can heal you

-true healing

true, lasting happiness;

it may not appear in a day
but you will work towards it
until one day
you wake up
without problems or cares
in pure bliss

-the day will come, stay strong

what is the point
of loving someone
whose heart
still belongs
to someone else?

-broken hearted

i used to thank god
every day
that i had you

now i beg god
every day
that i may forget you.

-praying to forget

wipe your tears away
do not waste the present
crying over the past

-do not cry for dead roses

someone who will love you
for who you truly are
is always worth
the wait

-*worth the wait*

you are special
you are loved
you are appreciated
you are worth the wait

-do not forget what you are

broken hearts
speak a language
only understood
by others
in the same pain

-broken hearts only

X

chapter two

lessons

i have learned many things
in my time
on this earth

the most important
of which
is that
we are all the same
in more ways than we know
and we should love each other
for that reason

-lessons

love never dies.
it is only reborn.

when someone leaves your life
do not blame it on yourself

the universe took them out
of your life
for a reason

-be grateful

never be afraid
to cut toxic people
out of your life
for the sake
of your own happiness

-it's always worth it

never forget
that you
are
good enough.

-don't let anyone tell you otherwise

let today
be the dawn
of a new era
in your life

one of happiness
peace
love
and joy

-claim it and make it real

do not forget
to take your own advice

so often we can see
what others need
but are so blind
when it comes to ourselves

-take your own advice

do not resent yourself
for how slowly you are healing

it takes time
and you need to remember that.

-healing is a slow process

you can't convince people
to give you
the love you deserve

-the love you deserve

do not lose sight
of the future

you will
figure out
your life

it's just
a matter
of time

-a matter of time

the only one
who can stop you
from living up
to your full
potential

is

you.

take responsibility
but also
never forget
that not everything
is your fault.

-responsibility

a loyal friend
is such a rarity

if you are lucky enough
to find such a person

hold on to them
and never let go

-loyalty is rare

to my father
who always provided for us
and put aside his own desires
so that we could have
everything we needed

you were the strongest man
i have ever known
and i hope i live up
to your memory.

-in honor of a great man

even if you don't agree
with the opinions
of others

it's important
to respect
their right
to believe what they want
and act how they want

-respect

take notice
when others
are honest
even when they do not
have to be

keep them around
for they will keep you
tied down to earth
when great winds prevail

-anchors

crying
is never weakness

-let it all out

it sucks going through things
and knowing
that someone
you used to lean on
for support
is no longer around
to do so...

-leaning on nothing

you may be tired
and lonely
and hurt

but take a breath
meditate
relax

you will find
your balance
again.

-balance

it was never
supposed
to end
this way

-tragedy

if you feel
that you
are not good enough

remember how far
you have come
and so hard it was
at the time

you will make it through this
just like you've made it
through everything else
that has come before.

-good enough

never forget
that other people
have their own wounds
their own stories
and their own pain

-be gentle

do not hurt others
in the same way
you've been hurt before

instead, love others
in the same ways
that others hurt you

in loving others
you will find the strength
to erase the past.

-erase the past

x

chapter three

comfort

beware of people
who try
to make you think
you aren't worth
their time

-you are worth it

deciding to move on
is the hardest part

-moving on

never forget
that the way you treat others
is like a pebble
thrown into the ocean

the tiniest waves
change the course
of history

-spread love

never forget
your own
value.

-value

do not allow others
to tell you
you aren't good enough

-you are

your potential
is limitless;

if only
you can
see it.

-potential

hold your head up high
you will get
through this

things will make sense
and you will only be
stronger
as a result of your trials.

-tribulations

the most important thing
is to never
give up
on yourself.

as long as you keep
believing
in yourself
and your potential

you will reach
what you desire
and much, much more.

-more

your resilience
to keep getting back up
when you fall down
is what moves you
forward

in life

-resilience

stop questioning
your instincts
and start following them

-compass

every word of love
and compassion
you utter

makes a difference
in others' lives

-be the change

you cannot tell the world
what to be
unless you are that thing
yourself

-be an example

beware of people
who find it easy
to walk away

-they will walk out on you too

you may think
that you don't have much

but try giving a compliment
to a stranger
or comforting
a friend

you see, in truth
you have all the power in the world
with only your words.

-words

choose
to be the one
to be the light
in someone else's darkness

-choose to be the light

loving others
teaches you
to love
yourself

-love yourself

the greater
your current struggle
the greater
the light is
at the end
of the tunnel

-tunnel

your future
is bright
and everything
will turn out
okay

-future

live one day
at a time

one hour
one minute
one moment
at a time

do not worry
what it all adds up to

only live
in the moment.

-moment

watch the way
you talk about yourself.

the way you speak of yourself
becomes your reality

so sow seeds of joy
instead of sadness

and watch them bloom
as time goes on.

-seeds of joy

it is okay to admit
to yourself
that you aren't okay.

X

chapter four

healing

broken hearts
don't have to
stay that way.

-one day at a time

how are you supposed
to follow your heart
when it is broken and bleeding?

sometimes the pain
of not being loved back
by someone you love
hurts more
than any physical pain
ever could

-pain

if someone treats you
like you're just another option
teach them
that you aren't.

-you are not just another option

don't spend your life
waiting
for an apology
that will never come.

move on
and accept the fact
that sometimes
closure never comes.

-closure

beware those
who only take from you
and never give back.

generosity is a good thing
but don't be a fool
and give everything
to someone
who will willingly take it all
and give you nothing in return.

-be vigilant

we are all just addicted
to the idea
that somehow love
could erase all our pain
and heal all of our wounds

-but only you can heal yourself

to be happy
means
being
at peace
with yourself.

-peace

do not just accept
the negativity of life

you have the ability
to fight it
and not let it
steal your joy

-fight back

do not expect
anyone
to forgive you
if you have not yet
forgiven
yourself

-forgive yourself

to live
a life
of positivity
you must surround yourself
with positive people

-positivity spreads

the art
of letting go
is simple

before you can let go
you have to examine
why you feel the need
to keep holding on

realize that you are looking
for a lifeline
only because
you are too afraid
to swim

-swim on

surround yourself
with positive energy
and cut off those
with toxicity

you are better off
without them

-*toxic*

we are only
searching for things
in others
that we wish we had
ourselves

-looking for love

my soul
laid bare
on parchment

-take what you want from me

find the light
within yourself
and set it free

-happiness

do not try so hard
to help others
that you forget
your own needs

-you cannot save others if you're dead

get out of your patterns
subvert your own habits

make yourself live life
as if it is new

that is the secret
to finding peace

-finding peace

don’t waste “i love you’s”
on people
who don’t understand
what that truly means

-true love

there will always be
another chance
to not repeat
your mistakes

the greatest joy
is in realizing
that your broken heart
finally doesn't hurt
anymore

-freedom always comes

thank you for reading my second collection of poetry. I hope that it gave you a little more life, light, and love.

-brandon helms

Lightning Source UK Ltd.
Milton Keynes UK
UKHW01f1821040618
323724UK00001B/317/P

9 781981 953493